This book belongs to:
这本图画书属于：

The Emperor of Absurdia

小国王的梦

[英] 克里斯·瑞德尔 文·图

曙 光 译

The Emperor of Absurdia was having
the most extraordinary dream.

荒唐小国王做了一个很奇怪的梦。

All of a **sudden** he woke to the **hoots** of the sky fish nibbling the umbrella trees.

突然，他被飞天鱼咀嚼雨伞树的声音吵醒了。

He tumbled　他翻身

out of　掉下了

bed ...　床……

...into the arms
of the
Wardrobe
Monster.

……落到了
衣橱
怪物的
胳膊里。

The Wardrobe Monster
helped the Emperor get dressed—

衣橱怪物帮小国王穿衣服——

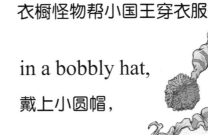

in a bobbly hat,
戴上小圆帽，

a crumply
coat,
穿上皱巴巴
的衣服，

and a pair of
jingle-jangle socks.
穿上一双叮叮当
的袜子。

"Have you seen my **snuggly scarf** anywhere?" the Emperor asked.
The Wardrobe Monster shook his big hairy head.

"你看见我那条羊毛围巾了吗?"小国王问。

衣橱怪物摇了摇他那颗长满头发的大脑袋。

"That's funny,
I had it yesterday,"
said the Emperor, and set off on a scarf hunt...

"太奇怪了,我昨天还戴了呢!"小国王一边说着一边出发去找围巾……

...whick took quite some time.　　……找了很长时间。

"It's no good," said the Emperor,
sitting under a pointy tree.
"I can't find my snuggly scarf
anywhere."

"真没用，"小国王坐在一棵
尖尖的树下说，"到处都找不
到我的羊毛围巾。"

Just then, from
the top of the
tree, there came a
loud, pointy-sounding
squawk.

正在这时，从树顶传来一
声呱呱的鸟叫声。

and there was his
**snuggly
scarf.**
那里面有他的
羊毛围巾。

and found a pointy nest…
发现了一个形状尖尖的鸟窝……

The Emperor climbed the pointy tree
小国王爬上尖尖的树顶，

The Emperor of
Absurdia put on his
scarf and went to
his high chair.

荒唐小国王围上围巾
爬上他高高的椅子。

Breakfast was served.

早餐已经端上来了。

And then **supper,**

晚餐之后

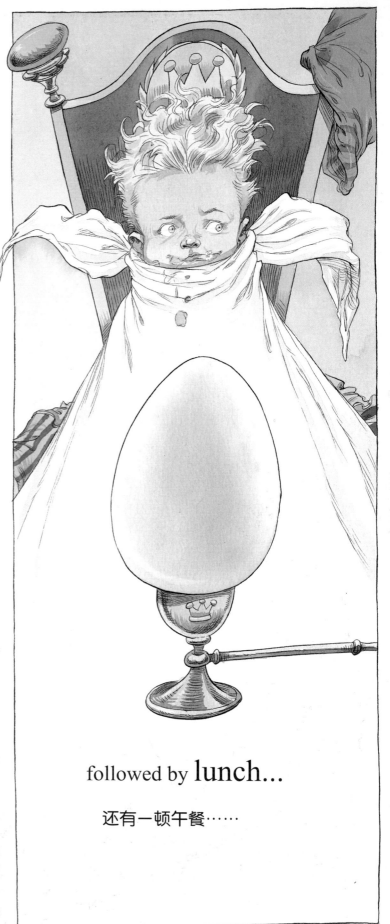

followed by **lunch...**

还有一顿午餐……

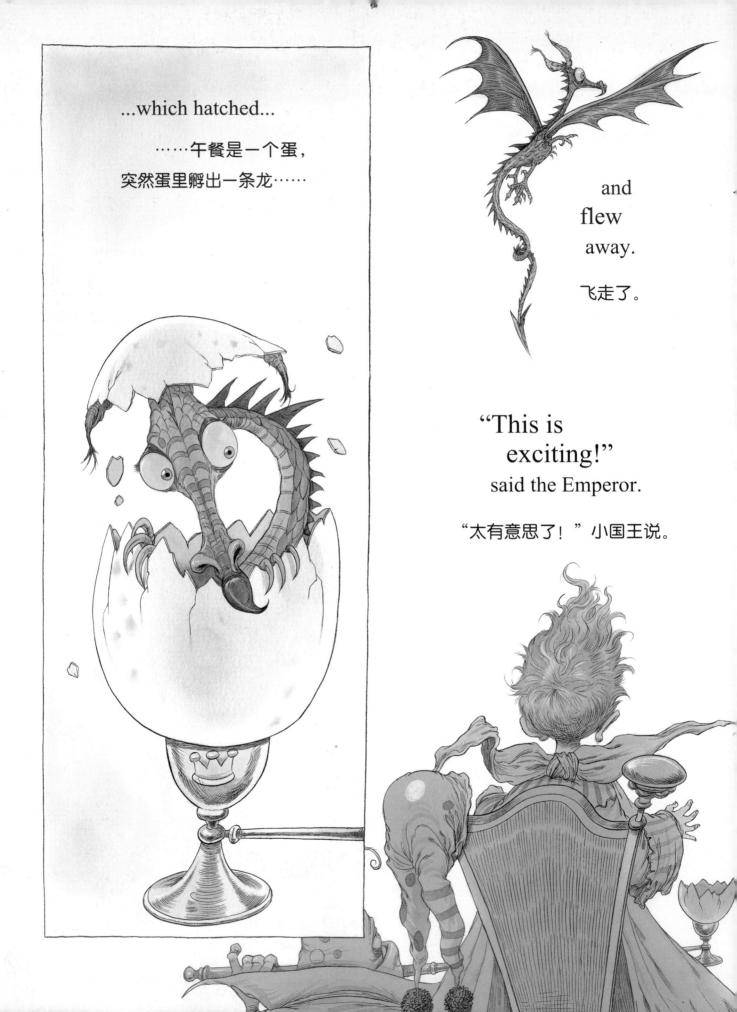

...which hatched...

……午餐是一个蛋，
突然蛋里孵出一条龙……

and
flew
away.

飞走了。

"This is
exciting!"
said the Emperor.

"太有意思了！"小国王说。

The Emperor of Absurdia called for his
tricycle chair
and set
off on a
dragon
hunt...

荒唐小国王坐
上他的三轮车去找
飞出去的龙……

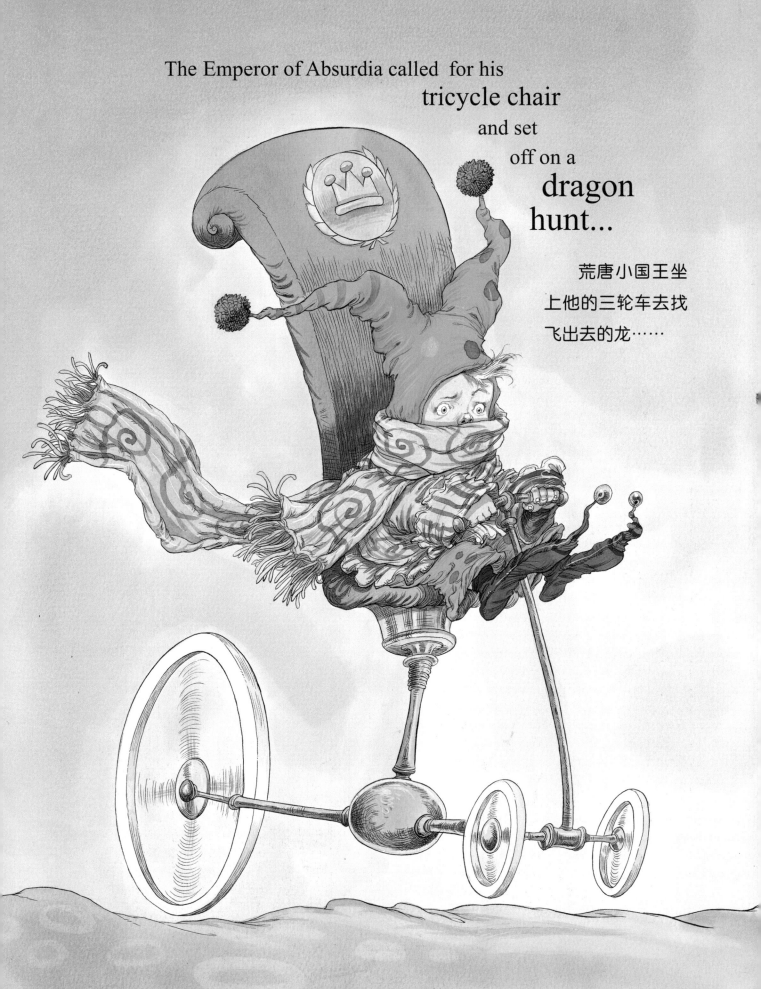

...Whick took quite some time.　　……这也花了不少时间。

He looked in the
flower beds
and up the
**umbrella
trees.**

他在花床中找，爬上
雨伞树找。

He looked
under
the **pillow
hills**

他在枕头山丘下找，

and over the bouncy mountains.
还在弹力山上找。

"It's no good," said the Emperor,
climbing down from his tricycle chair.
"I can't find the little dragon
anywhere."
"真没用，"小国王边说边爬下三轮车。
"我到处都找不到那只飞龙。"

He was just about
to give up, when he
noticed the footprints.

就在他正准备放弃的时候，
他发现了一些脚印。

They led into
a deep, dark
cave.

这些脚印一直延伸到
一个又深又黑的山洞前。

The Emperor took off his **bobbly hat** and his **jingle-jangle socks** and put them in the pocket of his **crumply coat.**

　　小国王摘下他的小圆帽，脱下他的叮叮当的袜子，把它们放在皱巴巴的衣服口袋里。

Then, as quietly as he could, he tiptoed inside the cave.

　　然后，他小心翼翼地踮着脚尖儿往山洞里走去。

And
out
again!

突然小国王
又
跑了出来！

"Help!" cried
the Emperor.
"An emperor hunt!"

"救命啊！"
小国王大喊。
"它要抓我！"

The dragon chased the Emperor across the bouncy mountains

飞龙紧紧地追赶小国王，追过弹力山，

and through the pillow hills,

追过枕头山丘，

under the umbrella trees and towards the flower beds.

追过雨伞树，向花床追去。

Then, just as
the dragon was
about to gobble
the Emperor up,
there came a loud,
pointy-sounding
squawk
and a pointy
bird swooped
down and
caught
hold of the
Emperor's
scarf.

就在飞龙要抓住小国王的时候，又传来了呱呱的鸟叫，
一只尖嘴鸟突然冲下来叼住小国王的围巾飞走了。

As they **flew** over the flower beds,
the Emperor let go of the scarf
and **tumbled**
down through
the air ...

就在他们飞过花床
的时候，小国王放
开了围巾从空中掉
了下来……

into the
arms of
the **Wardrobe**
Monster.

正好
落进了
衣橱怪物的
胳膊里。

He was
so pleased to
see the Emperor
that he gave him
an **extra**
big hug.

衣橱
怪物很高兴，
给了小国王
一个
大大的拥抱。

"I'll look
for my
snuggly scarf
tomorrow," said
the Emperor, and
the Wardrobe
Monster nodded
his big hairy head.

"我明天还要去找我
的羊毛围巾。"小国王说。
衣橱怪物点了点他那颗
长满头发的大脑袋。

Then, as a big buttercup moon rose in the sky, the Emperor of Absurdia **tumbled** into bed and fell fast asleep.

And as the sky fish **snored** in the umbrella trees ...

当奶油月亮高高地挂在天空的时候，荒唐小国王爬上床很快就睡着了。

飞天鱼也在雨伞树上打着呼噜……

... he had

the most

extraordinary

dream.

……这就是

小国王最

奇怪

的梦。

图书在版编目（CIP）数据

小国王的梦／（英）瑞德尔（Riddell,C.）编绘；
曙光译.—北京：中国电力出版社，2008
书名原文：The Emperor of Absurdia
ISBN 978-7-5083-7480-2

I.小… Ⅱ.①瑞…②曙… Ⅲ.图画故事－英国－
现代 I561.85

中国版本图书馆CIP数据核字（2008）第088800号

著作权合同登记号　　北京版权局图字：01-2008-1183

Text and Illustrations copyright © 2006 Chris Riddell

中国电力出版社出版、发行
电话：010-58383291 传真：010-58383291
（北京三里河路6号 100044 http：//www.ceppshaoer.com）
印刷：北京盛通印刷股份有限公司印刷
各地新华书店销售

2008年8月第一版　2008年8月 第一次印刷
889毫米 × 1194毫米 16开本 2印张 50千字
印数 0001 — 5000册 定价 13.90元

文　字：[英] 克里斯·瑞德尔
绘　画：[英] 克里斯·瑞德尔
翻　译：曙光
责任编辑：力荣
责任印制：陈焊彬

敬告读者
本书封面贴有防伪标签，加热后中心图案消失
本书如有印装质量问题，我社发行部负责退换
版权专有　翻印必究

 本书可配套九铭"点读机"点击发声
登陆 http://www.asiajiuming.com 了解更多信息